新雅兒童英文圖解字典

同義詞

Elaine Tin 著

receive

收到

get

新雅文化事業有限公司
www.sunya.com.hk

如何使用新雅點讀筆閱讀本書?

新雅‧點讀樂園 升級功能

讓孩子學習更輕鬆愉快!

本系列屬「新雅點讀樂園」產品之一,若配備新雅點讀筆,孩子可以點讀書中的字詞和相關例句的內容,聆聽英語和粵語,或是英語和普通話的發音。

想了解更多「新雅點讀樂園」產品,請瀏覽新雅網頁(www.sunya.com.hk)或掃描右邊的QR code進入 新雅‧點讀樂園。

Sun
太陽

1. 下載本書的點讀筆檔案

1 瀏覽新雅網頁(www.sunya.com.hk) 或掃描右邊的 QR code 進入 新雅·點讀樂園 。

2 點選 下載點讀筆檔案 ▶ 。

3 依照下載區的步驟說明，點選及下載《新雅兒童英文圖解字典》的點讀筆檔案至電腦，並複製至新雅點讀筆的「BOOKS」資料夾內。

2. 啟動點讀功能

開啟點讀筆後，請點選封面右上角的 新雅·點讀樂園 圖示，然後便可翻開書本，點選書本上字詞、圖畫或句子，點讀筆便會播放相應的內容。

3. 選擇語言

如想切換播放語言，請點選內頁右上角的圖示，當再次點選內頁時，點讀筆便會使用所選的語言播放點選的內容。

如何使用本字典？

　　《新雅兒童英文圖解字典：同義詞》適合幼稚園至初小學生，收錄超過180對同義詞。每個詞目均附英文詞性、中文釋義、漢語拼音、雙語例句，並配以精美插圖，內容清晰，一看就懂。

全書把同義詞分為10個主題，包括學習、家庭、健康、用餐、交通、休閒、感覺、工作、生活，以及程度。學童分類學習，事半功倍。

中文釋義上方提供漢語拼音，幫助孩子學習中文字詞的漢語發音。

學習

ENG 粵語　ENG × 普通話

class (n.)

kè táng
課堂

16

例句

We should pay attention in class.
我們應該專心上課。

利用新雅點讀筆點選圖示，可切換播放語言。

英文例句示範詞目的正確用法，中文翻譯方便讀者掌握意思。

詞目旁邊標示了詞性的縮寫，如下：

n.　　代表 noun（名詞）；
v.　　代表 verb（動詞）；
adj.　代表 adjective（形容詞）；
adv.　代表 adverb（副詞）；
prep.　代表 preposition（介詞）；
det.　代表 determiner（限定詞）。

本書為入門級的同義詞字典，旨在幫助學童掌握詞目的基本釋義，並建立其英文詞彙量。在內容編排上，每對同義詞均在同一個跨頁上呈現，左頁通常展示較顯淺容易的字詞，右頁則為意義相近但較為深奧的詞語。從左至右，由淺入深，孩子輕鬆學習英文詞彙。

左頁詞目較為顯淺，右頁詞目則是意義相近但較艱深的詞語，以易帶難，增加詞彙量。

英文字詞語義廣闊，而且一詞多義。即使兩個詞語意思相近，用法亦可有所不同。本書作為初階字典，會按需提供相關文字說明，並鼓勵讀者參考例句，配合語境，理解各詞目的語義和實際用法。

目錄

學習

class 課堂 / lesson （一節）課   16 - 17

easy 容易的 / simple 簡單的   18 - 19

explain 解釋 / clarify 闡釋   20 - 21

hard 困難的 / difficult 困難的   22 - 23

homework 功課 / schoolwork 學校課業   24 - 25

join 參加；加入 / participate 參加   26 - 27

learn 學習 / study 學習   28 - 29

line 隊伍 / queue 隊伍   30 - 31

mistake 錯誤 / error 錯誤   32 - 33

naughty 頑皮的 / mischievous 頑皮的   34 - 35

picture 圖片 / illustration 插圖   36 - 37

quiz 小測 / test 測驗   38 - 39

right 正確的 / correct 正確的   40 - 41

smart 聰明的 / clever 聰明的   42 - 43

student 學生 / pupil 學生   44 - 45

teach 教導 / instruct 指導   46 - 47

try 嘗試 / attempt 嘗試   48 - 49

understand 明白 / comprehend 理解   50 - 51

word 字詞 / vocabulary 詞語   52 - 53

家庭

adult 成人 / grown-up 成人	54 - 55
alike 相似的 / similar 相似的	56 - 57
annoying 令人煩厭的 / irritating 令人煩厭的	58 - 59
believe 相信 / trust 信任	60 - 61
child 小孩 / kid 小孩	62 - 63
comfortable 舒適的 / cozy 舒適的	64 - 65
family 家庭 / household 家庭；一戶人	66 - 67
help 幫助 / assist 幫助	68 - 69
hug 擁抱 / embrace 擁抱	70 - 71
live 居住 / dwell 居住	72 - 73
loving 有愛心的 / caring 有愛心的	74 - 75
party 派對 / gathering 聚會	76 - 77
politely 有禮貌地 / respectfully 恭敬地	78 - 79
put 放置 / place 放置	80 - 81
raise 養育 / nurture 養育	82 - 83
safe 安全的 / secure 安心的	84 - 85
sorry 抱歉的 / apologise 道歉	86 - 87
tidy 整潔的 / neat 整齊的	88 - 89
treasure 珍惜 / cherish 珍惜	90 - 91

健康

ache 痛 / pain 痛   92 - 93

cut 傷口 / wound 傷口   94 - 95

drug 藥物 / medicine 藥物   96 - 97

exercise 運動 / workout 運動訓練   98 - 99

fat 肥胖的 / chubby 胖乎乎的   100 - 101

flexible 靈活的 / agile 靈活的   102 - 103

healthy 健康的 / fit 健康的   104 - 105

hurt 受傷 / injure 受傷   106 - 107

nutritious 營養豐富的 / nourishing 營養豐富的   108 - 109

pill 藥丸 / tablet 藥丸   110 - 111

sick 生病的 / ill 生病的   112 - 113

soothe 紓緩 / relieve 緩解   114 - 115

strong 強壯的 / athletic 強壯的   116 - 117

thin 瘦削的 / slim 苗條的   118 - 119

tired 疲倦的 / exhausted 筋疲力竭的   120 - 121

treat 治療 / cure 治療   122 - 123

weak 體弱的 / fragile 虛弱的   124 - 125

用餐

aroma 香味 / scent 香味   126 - 127

beat 攪拌 / whisk 攪拌   128 - 129

can 罐頭 / tin 罐頭   130 - 131

candy 糖果 / sweet 糖果   132 - 133

clean 清潔的 / spotless 一塵不染的   134 - 135

congee 白粥 / porridge 燕麥粥   136 - 137

coupon 優惠券 / voucher 現金券   138 - 139

cut 切 / chop 切   140 - 141

drink 喝 / sip 啜飲   142 - 143

eat 吃 / have 吃   144 - 145

full 吃飽的 / stuffed 吃飽的   146 - 147

hot 辣的 / spicy 辣的   148 - 149

hungry 肚子餓的 / starving 飢餓的   150 - 151

oily 油膩的 / greasy 油膩的   152 - 153

salty 鹹的 / savoury 鹹的   154 - 155

seasoning 調味品 / condiment 調味品   156 - 157

taste 味道 / flavour 味道；口味   158 - 159

tasteless 沒味道的 / bland 淡而無味的   160 - 161

tasty 美味的 / delicious 美味的   162 - 163

uncooked 未經煮熟的 / raw 生的   164 - 165

✦ 交通

allow 允許 / permit 准許   166 - 167

bicycle 單車；自行車 / bike 單車；自行車   168 - 169

convenient 方便的 / accessible 容易到達的   170 - 171

crash 撞毀 / collide 相撞   172 - 173

crowded 擠迫的 / packed 擠迫的   174 - 175

empty 空的 / vacant 空的   176 - 177

fast 快速的 / quick 快速的   178 - 179

fly 飛翔 / glide 滑翔   180 - 181

forbid 禁止 / prohibit 禁止   182 - 183

jam 堵塞 / congestion 堵塞   184 - 185

leave 離開 / depart 離開   186 - 187

near 接近 / close 靠近   188 - 189

passenger 乘客 / traveller 旅客   190 - 191

reach 到達 / arrive 到達   192 - 193

rough 崎嶇的 / bumpy 顛簸的   194 - 195

sidewalk 行人道 / pavement 行人道   196 - 197

stop 車站 / station 車站   198 - 199

taxi 的士；計程車 / cab 的士；計程車   200 - 201

unsafe 不安全的 / dangerous 危險的   202 - 203

休閒

book 預訂 / reserve 預留　　　　　　　　　204 - 205

boring 沉悶的 / dull 無趣的　　　　　　　　206 - 207

browse 瀏覽 / surf 上網　　　　　　　　　　208 - 209

cartoon 卡通片 / animation 動畫　　　　　 210 - 211

exciting 刺激的 / thrillng 刺激的；驚險的　212 - 213

film 電影 / movie 電影　　　　　　　　　　214 - 215

free 空閒的 / spare 空餘的　　　　　　　　216 - 217

funny 有趣的 / amusing 有趣的　　　　　　218 - 219

game 比賽 / match 比賽　　　　　　　　　220 - 221

hobby 興趣；嗜好 / interest 興趣　　　　　222 - 223

holiday 假期 / vacation 假期　　　　　　　224 - 225

outdoor 室外的 / open-air 戶外的　　　　　226 - 227

photo 照片 / snapshot 照片　　　　　　　 228 - 229

relaxing 放鬆的 / chill 輕鬆的　　　　　　230 - 231

show 表演 / performance 表演　　　　　　232 - 233

trendy 時髦的 / fashionable 時尚的　　　　234 - 235

trip 旅程 / journey 旅程　　　　　　　　　236 - 237

感覺

angry 生氣的 / furious 憤怒的   238 - 239

beautiful 漂亮的 / pretty 漂亮的   240 - 241

brave 勇敢的 / courageous 勇敢的   242 - 243

calm 平靜的 / quiet 安靜的   244 - 245

compassionate 富同情心的 /   246 - 247
sympathetic 富同情心的

cute 可愛的 / lovely 可愛的   248 - 249

eager 熱切的 / enthusiastic 熱衷的   250 - 251

happy 快樂的 / cheerful 愉快的   252 - 253

hate 討厭 / dislike 討厭   254 - 255

honest 誠實的 / frank 坦誠的   256 - 257

jealous 妒忌的 / envious 羨慕的   258 - 259

kind 體貼的 / considerate 體貼的   260 - 261

mean 刻薄的 / unkind 刻薄的；無情的   262 - 263

nervous 緊張的 / anxious 焦慮的   264 - 265

sad 傷心的 / unhappy 不開心的   266 - 267

scared 害怕的 / afraid 害怕的   268 - 269

shy 害羞的 / timid 羞怯的   270 - 271

strange 奇怪的 / weird 怪異的   272 - 273

工作

ask 要求 / request 要求 274 - 275

boss 老闆 / employer 僱主 276 - 277

busy 忙碌的 / hectic 繁忙的 278 - 279

co-worker 同事 / colleague 同事 280 - 281

customer 顧客 / client 客戶 282 - 283

finish 完成 / complete 完成 284 - 285

found 創辦 / establish 創立 286 - 287

hardworking 勤奮的 / diligent 勤奮的 288 - 289

job 工作 / occupation 職業 290 - 291

meeting 會議 / conference 會議 292 - 293

salary 薪金 / wage 工資 294 - 295

search 尋找 / seek 尋找 296 - 297

send 發送 / deliver 遞送 298 - 299

show 展示 / demonstrate 展示 300 - 301

start 開始 / begin 開始 302 - 303

stress 壓力 / pressure 壓力 304 - 305

suggest 建議 / advise 建議 306 - 307

tell 告訴 / inform 通知 308 - 309

生活

buy 購買 / purchase 購買   310 - 311

cheap 便宜的 / inexpensive 價錢不貴的   312 - 313

choose 選擇 / select 挑選   314 - 315

cold 寒冷的 / chilly 寒冷的   316 - 317

collect 收集 / gather 收集   318 - 319

dawn 黎明 / daybreak 黎明   320 - 321

disturb 干擾 / interrupt 打斷   322 - 323

expensive 昂貴的 / pricey 昂貴的   324 - 325

fix 修理 / repair 維修   326 - 327

friend 朋友 / pal 朋友   328 - 329

get 收到 / receive 收到   330 - 331

hope 希望 / wish 希望   332 - 333

provide 提供 / offer 提供   334 - 335

refuse 拒絕 / reject 拒絕   336 - 337

rich 富有的 / wealthy 富有的   338 - 339

talk 談話 / speak 說話   340 - 341

want 想要 / desire 渴求   342 - 343

wet 濕的 / humid 潮濕的   344 - 345

程度

almost 幾乎 / **nearly** 差不多   346 - 347

big 大的 / **large** 大的   348 - 349

each 每一個 / **every** 每一個   350 - 351

enough 足夠 / **sufficient** 充足的   352 - 353

formerly 之前 / **previously** 之前   354 - 355

last 最後的 / **final** 最後的   356 - 357

many 很多 / **numerous** 很多的   358 - 359

new 全新的 / **unused** 沒用過的   360 - 361

next 下一個的 / **following** 下一個的   362 - 363

often 時常 / **regularly** 經常   364 - 365

reduce 減少 / **decrease** 減少   366 - 367

same 相同的 / **identical** 一模一樣的   368 - 369

second-hand 二手的 / **pre-owned** 二手的   370 - 371

seldom 很少 / **rarely** 很少   372 - 373

small 小的 / **little** 小的   374 - 375

soon 即將 / **shortly** 不久   376 - 377

whole 整個的 / **entire** 整個的   378 - 379

wide 寬闊的 / **broad** 寬闊的   380 - 381

class (n.)

kè táng
課堂

 例句 -

We should pay attention in class.

我們應該專心上課。

lesson (n.)

yì jié kè

（一節）課

17

 例句 -

I have piano lessons on Wednesdays.

我逢星期三要上鋼琴課。

easy (adj.)

róng yì de
容易的

 例句

- -

Spelling is easy if you know how to break words into syllables.

如果懂得把單字拆成音節，拼寫是很容易的。

18

simple (adj.)

jiǎn dān de
簡單的

 例句

Single-digit addition is very simple.

單位數加法是很簡單的。

explain (v.)

jiě shì

解釋

20

 例句 -

The teacher is explaining how to do the sum.

老師正在解釋如何計算這道數學題。

clarify (v.)

chǎn shì

闡釋

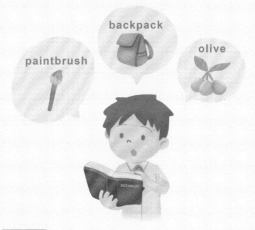

backpack

paintbrush

olive

 例句

A dictionary is used for clarifying the meaning of words.

字典的用途是闡釋字詞的意思。

hard (adj.)

kùn　nan　de
困難的

 例句 -

This article is too hard for primary school students.

這篇文章對小學生來說太難了。

difficult (adj.)

kùn nan de

困難的

 例句

Dictation may be difficult, but it is important for language learners.

默書或許很困難，但是對學習語文的人來說，是很重要的。

homework (n.)

gōng kè
功課

24

 例句 -----------------------------

My elder brother always helps me with my homework.

哥哥經常教我做功課。

schoolwork (n.)

xué xiào kè yè
學校課業

 例句 ----------------------------

Schoolwork helps students review what they have learned.

學校課業能幫助學生溫習學過的知識。

join (v.)

cān jiā　jiā rù
參加；加入

 例句 -----------------------------

We are going to play basketball. Do you want to join us?

我們現在去打籃球，你要和我們一起嗎？

participate (v.)

cān jiā
參加

 例句 ----------------------------

She loves singing. She has participated in her school choir since she was six.

她熱愛唱歌。自六歲開始,她就參加了學校的合唱團。

learn (v.)

xué xí

學習

28

 例句 ----------------------------

We can learn a lot about nature on a field trip.

我們可以在戶外考察中學習很多大自然知識。

study (v.)

xué xí
學習

 例句 - - - - - - - - -

study 也可指「修讀」。

29

My elder sister studies music at university.
姊姊在大學修讀音樂。

學習

line (n.)

duì wu
隊伍

例句

You need to get in line and wait for your turn to use the computer.

你要排隊，等候輪到你時才使用電腦。

queue (n.)

duì wu
隊伍

 例句 -

There is a long queue for the toilet.
洗手間有很多人排隊。

mistake (n.)

cuò wù
錯誤

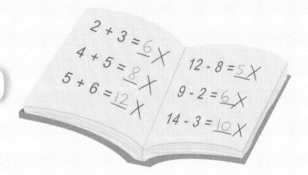

32

 例句 ----------------------------

To avoid careless mistakes, you should double-check your calculations.

為了避免大意的錯誤，你應該複查算式。

error (n.)

cuò wù
錯誤

33

 例句 -

He made a lot of capitalisation errors in his writing.

他的文章犯了很多字母大寫的錯誤。

ENG × 粵語

ENG × 普通話

naughty (adj.)

wán pí de
頑皮的

 例句 -

The naughty boys are running and shouting loudly in the corridor.

這羣頑皮的男孩在走廊上奔跑和尖叫。

mischievous (adj.)

wán pí de
頑皮的

例句

The mischievous boy got detention for playing tricks on his classmate.

這個頑皮的男孩捉弄同學，所以被罰留堂。

picture (n.)

tú piàn
圖片

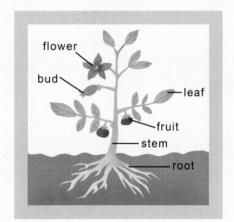

flower

bud

leaf

fruit

stem

root

 例句 -

The picture clearly shows the different parts of a plant.

這幅圖片清楚展示植物的不同部分。

36

illustration (n.)

chā tú
插圖

 例句

The illustrations in this book help us understand the story better.

書中的插圖幫助我們更容易理解故事內容。

quiz (n.)

xiǎo cè
小測

Quiz 1

Name:
Date:
Marks:

1. ～～? ＿＿ 11. ～～? ＿＿
2. ～～? ＿＿ 12. ～～～? ＿＿
3. ～～～? ＿＿ 13. ～～～? ＿＿
4. ～～? ＿＿ 14. ～～～? ＿＿
5. ～～? ＿＿ 15. ～～～? ＿＿
6. ～～～? ＿＿ 16. ～～～? ＿＿
7. ～～? ＿＿ 17. ～～～? ＿＿
8. ～～? ＿＿ 18. ～～～? ＿＿
9. ～～～? ＿＿ 19. ～～～? ＿＿
10. ～～～? ＿＿ 20. ～～～? ＿＿

 例句 -

The quiz has twenty questions.

小測共有二十道題目。

test (n.)

cè yàn

測驗

 例句 -

The test was so easy. Everyone got good marks.

這次測驗非常容易，每位同學都取得高分。

right (adj.)

zhèng què de
正確的

40

 例句 -

Ms Chan is showing us the right way to hold a pencil.

陳老師正在向我們示範正確的執筆方法。

correct (adj.)

zhèng què de
正確的

 例句

In the quiz competition, we can get five marks for each correct answer.

在問答比賽中，每個正確答案可得五分。

smart (adj.)

cōng míng de
聰明的

 例句 -

She has solved all the riddles. How smart she is!

她猜對所有謎語,真聰明!

clever (adj.)

cōng míng de
聰明的

 例句 --------------------------------

Mark is so clever that he has built the robot on his own.

馬克很聰明，他自己製作了一個機械人。

ENG × 粵語

ENG × 普通話

student (n.)

xué sheng

學生

 例句

The students are decorating the notice board in their classroom.

學生正在布置教室內的壁報板。

44

pupil (n.)

xué sheng
學生

45

 例句

pupil 尤指小學生。

The pupils are listening to their teacher attentively.

學生正在專心地聆聽老師講課。

teach (v.)

jiào dǎo
教導

 例句 -

Ms Wong will teach us Chinese this school year.

黃老師在本學年會任教我們中文科。

instruct (v.)

zhǐ dǎo
指導

 例句 ----------------------------

The coach is instructing us to grip a badminton racket.

教練正在指導我們握好羽毛球拍。

try (n.)

cháng shì
嘗試

48

 例句 ----------------------------

It looks fun. Let's give it a try!

這看起來很好玩。我們嘗試一下吧！

attempt (n.)

cháng shì
嘗試

 例句

At his third attempt, he finally won the interclass writing contest.

經過三次嘗試，他終於在班際寫作比賽中獲勝。

understand (v.)

<ruby>明<rt>míng</rt></ruby><ruby>白<rt>bai</rt></ruby>

50

 例句

The experiment helps us understand magnetism.

這個實驗讓我們明白什麼是磁力。

comprehend (v.)

lǐ jiě
理解

51

 例句

He does not know enough words to comprehend this text.

他認識的字詞太少了，不足以理解這篇課文。

word (n.)

zì cí
字詞

52

 例句 ----------------------------

If you want to find the meaning of a word, you can look it up in a dictionary.

如果想知道字詞的意思，可以去查看字典。

vocabulary (n.)

cí yǔ
詞語

mirror

candlestick

rose

53

例句

Reading is a good way to expand your vocabulary.

閱讀是增加詞彙量的好方法。

adult (n.)

chéng rén
成人

 例句 -

Children should not be left alone at home. They should be accompanied by an adult.

小孩子不應獨留家中，他們應該由成人陪伴看管。

grown-up (n.)

chéng rén

成人

 例句 ----------------------------

You should ask a grown-up to help you if you want to use a knife.

如果你想用刀，就應該請成人來幫忙。

alike (adj.)

xiāng shì de
相似的

56

 例句 --------- | alike 多用於形容樣貌。

My elder brother and I look very alike.
Our relatives sometimes mix us up.

哥哥和我長得很相似，親戚有時會把我們認錯。

similar (adj.)

xiāng shì de
相似的

 例句 ----------------------------

My elder sister and I have similar hairstyles.
姊姊和我的髮型很相似。

annoying (adj.)

lìng rén fán yàn de
令人煩厭的

 例句

Although my baby sister is very cute, she is annoying when she cries.

雖然我的小妹妹很可愛，但是她哭鬧時很令人煩厭。

irritating (adj.)

lìng rén fán yàn de
令人煩厭的

 例句 --------------------------------

Mark and Matt always quarrel with each other. It is so irritating.

馬克和馬特經常吵架,真令人煩厭。

believe (v.)

xiāng xìn
相信

60

 例句 -

He says he waters the plant every day but mum does not believe him.

他說他每天都有澆水，但是媽媽不相信他。

trust (v.)

xìn rèn
信任

61

 例句 -

I trust my mum the most because she always loves me.

我最信任媽媽，因為她永遠愛護我。

child (n.)

xiǎo hái
小孩

 例句

Although he is the only child, he has many cousins and he never feels lonely.

雖然他是獨生子，但是他有很多表兄弟姊妹，從不感到寂寞。

kid (n.)

xiǎo hái
小孩

 例句 ----------------------------

Mr Wong has three kids.

黃先生有三個孩子。

comfortable (adj.)

shū shì de
舒適的

 例句 ----------------------------

My new pillow is so soft and comfortable.

我的新枕頭很柔軟舒適。

64

cozy (adj.)

shū shì de
舒適的

 例句 ------------------------

After dinner, we all sit on the cozy sofa and enjoy the movie.

吃過晚飯後，我們坐在舒適的沙發上，享受看電影的時光。

family (n.)

jiā tíng
家庭

 例句

Chinese New Year is the festival for family reunions.

農曆新年是一家人團聚的節日。

household (n.)

jiā tíng yí hù rén
家庭；一戶人

 例句 -------------------------------

Children should take part in some household chores.

小朋友應該做一些家務。

help (v.)

bāng zhù
幫助

 例句 -

Mum is folding the clothes and I am helping her with it.

媽媽正在摺疊衣服，我正在幫助她。

assist (v.)

bāng zhù
幫助

 例句 - - - - - - - - - -

> assist 也可指「協助；緩助」。

My little brother is eager to assist dad in fixing the car.

弟弟渴望幫助爸爸維修汽車。

hug (n.)

yōng bào
擁抱

70

 例句 -

My dad gives me a big hug when he comes back home every day.

爸爸每天回家後，都會給我一個大大的擁抱。

embrace (n.)

yōng bào
擁抱

 例句 --------------------------

Aunt Mary greeted us with a warm embrace.

瑪莉姨姨以温暖的擁抱迎接我們。

live (v.)

jū zhù
居住

 例句 -

My aunt's family and my family live in the same neighbourhood.

姨姨一家和我們一家住在同一區。

dwell (v.)

jū zhù
居住

 例句

Our grandparents dwell in the country.

祖父母在鄉村居住。

ENG × 粵語   ENG × 普通話

loving (adj.)

yǒu ài xīn de
有愛心的

74

 例句 -

The loving girl is making a birthday card for her grandmother.

這位很有愛心的女孩正在製作生日卡給祖母。

caring (adj.)

yǒu ài xīn de
有愛心的

 例句 -

Jenny is a very caring sister. She holds her little brother's hand all the time.

珍妮是一位很有愛心的姊姊，她總是牽着弟弟的手。

party (n.)

pài duì
派對

 例句 --------------------------------

My parents will throw me a birthday party at home.

父母會在家中為我舉辦生日派對。

gathering (n.)

jù huì
聚會

 例句 -

We usually have festive gatherings at our grandparents' home.

我們通常會在祖父母家舉辦節日聚會。

politely (adv.)

yǒu lǐ mào de
有禮貌地

Could someone help me, please?

 例句 -

To ask for help politely, you should say "please".

請求別人幫忙時，應該要有禮貌地說「請」。

respectfully (adv.)

gōng jìng de
恭敬地

 例句

Gavin received the red packets from his grandparents respectfully.

加文恭敬地接過祖父母的紅封包。

put (v.)

fàng zhì
放置

 例句 ----------------------------

Mum asked me to put my toys into the box.

媽媽叫我把玩具放進箱子裏。

place (v.)

fàng　zhì
放置

 例句 -

Dad placed the lamp on the side table.

爸爸把枱燈放在茶几上。

raise (v.)

<ruby>養<rt>yǎng</rt></ruby> <ruby>育<rt>yù</rt></ruby>

例句 ----------------------------

I was raised in a big family.

我在一個大家庭中成長。

nurture (v.)

yǎng yù
養育

83

 例句 - - - - - - - - -

> nurture 也可指「培育；培養」。

Susan quit her work to nurture her children.

蘇珊辭去工作，養育孩子。

safe (adj.)

ān quán de
安全的

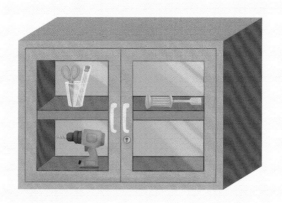

 例句 - - - - - - - - - - - - - - - - - -

To keep home safe, sharp objects should be kept in places that children cannot reach.

為保障家居安全,尖銳物品要安放在孩子觸及不到的地方。

secure (adj.)

ān xīn de
安心的

 例句 -----------------------------

The newborn baby feels secure when his mother is holding him.

初生嬰兒被媽媽抱住,感到很安心。

sorry (adj.)

bào qiàn de
抱歉的

86

 例句 -

Mum, I broke the vase. I am sorry.

媽媽，我把花瓶打破了，對不起。

apologise (v.)

dào qiàn
道歉

 例句 -

Terry, you shouldn't have pulled your little sister's hair. You should apologise to her.

托里，你不應該拉扯妹妹的頭髮，你要向她道歉。

tidy (adj.)

zhěng jié de
整潔的

 例句

Mum always keeps our home tidy.

媽媽經常把家裏收拾得很整潔。

neat (adj.)

zhěng qí de
整齊的

 例句

My little sister puts her dolls in a neat row.
妹妹把洋娃娃整整齊齊排成一列。

treasure (v.)

zhēn xī
珍惜

例句

John treasures every toy car given by his grandpa.

約翰珍惜每一輛祖父送的玩具車。

cherish (v.)

zhēn xī
珍惜

例句

Mum cherishes her kids' childhood. She keeps their photos in a nice album.

媽媽珍惜孩子的童年，把他們的照片收藏在精美的相簿內。

ache (n.)

tòng
痛

 例句 - - - - - - - - - - -

ache 尤指持續的疼痛。

I am having a stomach ache. I need to go to the toilet now.

我肚子痛，現在要上廁所。

pain (n.)

tòng
痛

 例句 -

Poor posture can cause back pain.

不良姿勢會導致背部疼痛。

cut (n.)

shāng kǒu
傷口

94

 例句 - - - - - - - - - - - -

cut 還有其他意思，
請參看第140頁。

This plaster can fit the cut on your finger.

這塊膠布貼合你手指上的傷口。

wound (n.)

shāng kǒu
傷口

 例句 -

The nurse is cleaning his wound.

護士正在為他清潔傷口。

drug (n.)

yào wù
藥物

 例句 - - - - - - - - - -

drug 也可指「毒品」。

These drugs have expired. We should throw them away.

這些藥物過期了，我們應該丟棄它們。

medicine (n.)

yào wù
藥物

97

 例句 --------------------------------

You may feel drowsy after taking this medicine.

服用這種藥物後，你可能會感到昏昏欲睡。

exercise (n.)

yùn dòng
運動

 例句

Regular exercise is important for our health.

恆常運動對我們的健康很重要。

workout (n.)

yùn dòng xùn liàn
運動訓練

 例句

Look at my muscles! My workouts are really paying off.

看看我的肌肉！運動訓練真的很有成效。

fat (adj.)

féi pàng de
肥胖的

 例句 -

I look so fat. I think I need to eat less.

我看起來很肥胖，我想我要少吃一點東西。

chubby (adj.)

pàng hū hū de
胖乎乎的

 例句

Fitness training is rather challenging for these chubby children.

對這羣胖乎乎的小朋友來說，體能訓練相當有挑戰性。

flexible (adj.)

líng huó de
靈活的

 例句 -

She has practised yoga for many years.
She has a flexible body.

她練習瑜伽多年，身體很靈活。

agile (adj.)

líng huó de
靈活的

103

 例句 - - - - - - - -

agile 也可指「敏捷的」。

The gymnast is very agile. He can do many difficult moves.

這位體操運動員身手靈活，能做出多種高難度動作。

healthy (adj.)

jiàn kāng de
健康的

104

 例句 ----------------------------

If you want to stay healthy, you should eat more vegetables and fruit.

如果想保持身體健康，就應該多吃蔬菜和水果。

fit (adj.)

jiàn kāng de
健康的

 例句 -

**She goes jogging every morning to keep
fit.**

她每天早上都會慢跑，保持身體健康。

hurt (v.)

shòu shāng

受傷

  例句 ----------------------

He hurt his elbow when he fell off the ladder.

他從梯子摔下來，弄傷了手肘。

injure (v.)

shòu shāng
受傷

 例句 -----------------------------

She tripped over a stone and injured her knees.

她被石頭絆倒，跌傷了膝蓋。

nutritious (adj.)

yíng yǎng fēng fù de
營養豐富的

 例句 -

Nuts like almonds, pistachios and walnuts are a great choice of nutritious snacks.

杏仁、開心果和核桃等堅果都是營養豐富的小吃。

ENG × 粵語 ENG × 普通話

nourishing (adj.)

yíng yǎng fēng fù de
營養豐富的

109

 例句 ----------------------------

This nourishing salad contains chicken, kale and tomatoes.

這碗營養豐富的沙律有雞肉、羽衣甘藍和番茄。

✏ salad 的普通話是「沙拉」。

pill (n.)

yào wán
藥丸

 例句 -

I prefer fresh fruit and vegetables rather than vitamin pills.

相比服用維他命丸，我寧願進食新鮮水果和蔬菜。

tablet (n.)

yào wán
藥丸

 例句 ------------------------------

You may dissolve the tablet in warm water before taking it.

你可以先把藥丸溶於暖水中，然後才服用。

sick (adj.)

shēng bìng de
生病的

112

例句 -

You have a fever. You need to take a sick leave today.

你發燒了，你今天要請病假。

ill (adj.)

shēng bìng de

生病的

113

✨ 例句 ----------------------

I am ill with the flu. I cannot go out with you.

我患了流感，不能跟你外出。

soothe (v.)

shū huǎn
紓緩

例句 -

A glass of warm water with honey may soothe your sore throat.

一杯溫暖的蜜糖水可以紓緩喉嚨痛。

114

relieve (v.)

huǎn jiě
緩解

115

例句 -

I gave mum a massage to relieve the tension in her shoulders.

我為媽媽按摩，以緩解她肩膊的繃緊。

strong (adj.)

qiáng zhuàng de
強壯的

116

 例句 -

He is so strong that he can lift the rock easily.

他體格強壯，能輕易搬起石頭。

athletic (adj.)

qiáng zhuàng de
強 壯 的

 例句 - - - - - - - - - -

> athletic 也可指「運動員的；田徑運動的」。

They are very athletic. It is hopeless to beat them.

他們太強壯了，要打敗他們是毫無希望的。

117

thin (adj.)

shòu xuē de

瘦削的

118

 例句 -

You are too thin. You should eat more.

你太瘦了，你應該多吃一點東西。

slim (adj.)

miáo tiao de
苗條的

 例句 -

To keep her slim figure, she is very careful of what she eats.

為了保持苗條的身形，她很小心選擇食物。

tired (adj.)

pí juàn de
疲倦的

例句

She always feels tired after work.

她下班後總是感到很疲倦。

exhausted (adj.)

jīn pí lì jié de
筋疲力竭的

 例句

He was exhausted by the time he finished the marathon.

他跑完馬拉松後，筋疲力竭了。

treat (v.)

zhì liáo

治療

122

 例句 -

Many plants can be used to treat illnesses.

很多植物都可以用來治療疾病。

cure (v.)

zhì liáo

治療

 例句 -

Taking enough rest is a good way to cure a cold.

充分休息對治療感冒很有用。

weak (adj.)

tǐ ruò de
體弱的

124

✨ 例句 -

He is too weak to move this box.
他體弱無力得連這個箱子都搬不動。

fragile (adj.)

xū ruò de
虛弱的

 例句 -

No wonder the old lady looks fragile —
she is 101 years old.

這位老太太已經101歲了，難怪她看起來很
虛弱。

aroma (n.)

xiāng wèi
香味

126

 例句

Once I got home, I could smell the aroma from the kitchen.

我一回到家，就聞到從廚房傳來的香味。

scent (n.)

xiāng wèi
香味

 例句 --------------------------

The scent of the lavender tea filled the air.

空氣中瀰漫薰衣草茶散發的香味。

beat (v.)

jiǎo bàn

攪拌

128

例句 -

Mum is beating the egg with chopsticks.

媽媽正在用筷子打勻雞蛋。

whisk (v.)

jiǎo bàn
攪拌

 例句 ----------------------

Be patient! It takes a few minutes to whisk the egg whites until you have stiff peaks.

耐心點！把蛋白打發成挺身的蛋白霜，需要幾分鐘時間。

129

egg white的普通話是「蛋清」。

can (n.)

guàn tou
罐頭

130

 例句

We store many cans of soup in our cupboard.

我們存放了很多罐頭湯在櫥櫃裏。

tin (n.)

guàn tou
罐頭

 例句 -

Whenever we have no idea what to eat,
we open a tin of beans.

每當我們想不到吃什麼時，就會開一罐豆來吃。

candy (n.)

táng guǒ
糖果

 例句 -

The fruity candies are colourful.

這些水果味糖果顏色繽紛。

sweet (n.)

táng guǒ
糖果

133

 例句 -

He gave his friend a packet of sweets yesterday.

昨天他送了一包糖果給朋友。

clean (adj.)

qīng jié de
清潔的

 例句 -

Clean drinking water is very precious so we must not waste it.

潔淨的飲用水十分珍貴，我們一定不能浪費。

spotless (adj.)

yì chén bù rǎn de
一塵不染的

 例句 -

The chef requires the staff to keep the kitchen spotless.

大廚要求員工保持廚房一塵不染。

congee (n.)

bái zhōu
白粥

 例句

Congee is made with rice. It is a traditional Chinese dish.

白粥用白米煮成，是一種傳統的中國食物。

porridge (n.)

yàn mài zhōu
燕麥粥

 例句 - - - - - - - - - - - - - - - -

She makes porridge with milk and bananas.
她用牛奶和香蕉煮燕麥粥。

coupon (n.)

yōu huì quàn
優惠券

138

 例句

You can get a free drink if you present this coupon at the counter.

在櫃枱出示這張優惠券，可以獲贈一杯飲品。

voucher (n.)

xiàn jīn quàn
現金券

 例句 ----------------

The voucher expires next week. Let's redeem a cake.

這張現金券下星期就到期了，我們去換一個蛋糕吧。

cut (v.)

qiè
切

 例句 - - - - - - - - - - - -

cut 還有其他意思，
請參看第94頁。

He asked dad to help him cut the lemon into slices so that he could make some lemonade.

他請爸爸幫他把檸檬切片，用來沖檸檬水。

chop (v.)

qiè
切

 例句 ----------

chop 多指切片、絲等。

The chef is chopping a thick piece of meat with a sharp carving knife.

大廚用鋒利的切肉刀切割一塊厚肉。

drink (v.)

hē

喝

142

 例句 -

I drink a glass of milk every morning.

我每天早上都喝一杯牛奶。

sip (v.)

chuò yǐn
啜飲

143

 例句 -----------------------------

Grandma is slowly sipping her hot tea.

祖母正在慢慢地呷熱茶。

eat (v.)

chī
吃

144

 例句 -------------------------

He eats a sandwich for breakfast every day.

他每天早餐都吃三文治。

sandwich 的普通話是「三明治」。

have (v.)

chī
吃

145

 例句 — — — — — — —

have 也可指「有；擁有」。

We will have seafood for dinner tonight.

今天晚餐我們會吃海鮮。

full (adj.)

chī bǎo de
吃飽的

例句 -

Everyone is so full after enjoying the feast.

享用過大餐後，大家都很飽。

stuffed (adj.)

chī bǎo de
吃飽的

 例句 -

I am stuffed. I cannot eat anymore.

我飽了,不能再吃了。

hot (adj.)

là de
辣的

148

 例句

The curry sauce is too hot for young children.

這款咖喱汁對小朋友來說太辣了。

spicy (adj.)

là de
辣的

149

 例句 -

The noodles were too spicy. He sweated a lot while eating them.

這碗麵太辣了。他一邊吃，一邊流汗。

hungry (adj.)

dǔ zi è de
肚子餓的

 例句 --------------------------------

He was so hungry that he gulped down the hotdog at once.

他肚子太餓了,一口氣就把熱狗吃完。

starving (adj.)

jī è de
飢餓的

 例句 ----------------------------

I did not have breakfast this morning.
I am starving now.

我今天早上沒有吃早餐，現在餓極了。

oily (adj.)

yóu nì de
油膩的

 例句

The chips are very oily. Don't eat too much.

這些薯條很油膩，不要吃太多。

greasy (adj.)

yóu nì de
油膩的

153

例句 -

The pizza is greasy. One slice is enough for me.

這個薄餅很油膩，我吃一塊就夠了。

salty (adj.)

xián de

鹹 的

154

 例句 -

Do not add too much soy sauce, otherwise the noodles will be too salty.

不要加太多醬油，否則麵會很鹹。

savoury (adj.)

xián de
鹹的

155

 例句 -

Pancakes taste very good with savoury ingredients like eggs and bacon.

厚煎餅配搭雞蛋和煙肉等鹹食材，真是美味。

seasoning (n.)

tiáo wèi pǐn
調味品

 例句 -

Mum cooks this delicious dish with
seasonings like herbs, garlic and honey.

媽媽用香草、蒜頭和蜜糖等調味品烹煮這道
菜式。

condiment (n.)

tiáo wèi pǐn
調味品

 例句 --------------------------------

Many restaurants provide condiments like salt and pepper at the table.

很多餐廳都在餐桌上放置鹽和胡椒等調味品。

taste (n.)

wèi dào
味道

158

 例句 -

I do not like the taste of blue cheese.
It is too strong.

我不喜歡藍芝士的味道，太濃烈了。

ENG × 粵語
ENG × 普通話

flavour (n.)

wèi dào　　kǒu wèi
味道；口味

159

例句 --------------------------------

Vanilla is one of the most popular ice cream flavours.

雲呢拿是最受歡迎的雪糕口味之一。

 vanilla 的普通話是「香草」。

tasteless (adj.)

méi wèi dào de
沒味道的

160

 例句 -

The soup is tasteless! Did you forget to add salt in it?

這碗湯沒有味道！你忘記了放鹽嗎？

bland (adj.)

dàn ér wú wèi de
淡而無味的

 例句

The bread is too bland. May I have some jam?

這片麵包淡而無味，可以給我一些果醬嗎？

tasty (adj.)

měi wèi de
美味的

162

 例句 -

This shop sells tasty cupcakes.

這間店舖售賣美味的紙杯蛋糕。

delicious (adj.)

měi wèi de
美味的

 例句 --------------------------

The fried chicken leg is delicious.

這件炸雞腿很美味。

uncooked (adj.)

wèi jīng zhǔ shú de
未經煮熟的

164

 例句

Uncooked meat may contain bacteria and cause food poisoning.

未經煮熟的肉類含有細菌，可引致食物中毒。

raw (adj.)

shēng de
生的

165

例句 ----------- raw 多用於形容食物。

Celery and cucumbers are vegetables that you can eat raw.

西芹和青瓜是可以生吃的蔬菜。

 cucumber 的普通話是「黃瓜」。

交通

allow (v.)

yǔn xǔ
允許

166

例句

Each passenger is allowed to carry a piece of small luggage.

每位乘客允許攜帶一件小型行李。

permit (v.)

zhǔn xǔ
准許

 例句

Only school buses are permitted to park in the school car park.

學校的停車場只准許校車停泊。

bicycle (n.)

dān chē　　　zì xíng chē
單車；自行車

168

✨ 例句 -------------------------------

He goes to school by bicycle every day.
他每天都騎單車上學。

 bicycle 的普通話是「自行車」。

bike (n.)

dān chē　　zì xíng chē
單車；自行車

 例句

We must not ride a bike on the pavement.

我們不能在行人路上騎單車。

✏ bike 的普通話是「自行車」。

convenient (adj.)

fāng biàn de
方便的

 例句

- -

It takes only five minutes to walk from my home to school. How convenient!

從我家步行到學校,只需要五分鐘,真方便!

accessible (adj.)

róng yì dào dá de
容易到達的

SHOPPING MALL

171

 例句

The location of the shopping mall is easily accessible by railway and bus.

這座購物商場位置便利，乘搭鐵路或巴士都可到達。

bus 的普通話是「公共汽車」。

crash (v.)

zhuàng huǐ
撞 毀

172

例句 -

Jack crashed his bike into a tree.

積克把單車撞到一棵樹上。

 bike 的普通話是「自行車」。

collide (v.)

xiāng zhuàng

相 撞

173

例句 -

A motorbike collided with a car.

一輛電單車和一輛汽車相撞。

motorbike 的普通話是「摩托車」。

crowded (adj.)

jǐ pò de
擠迫的

 例句

The train platform is very crowded during rush hour.

在繁忙時段，火車站月台非常擠迫。

packed (adj.)

jǐ pò de
擠迫的

例句

The bus is so packed that I cannot get onto it.

巴士太擠迫了，我上不了車。

bus 的普通話是「公共汽車」。

empty (adj.)

kōng de
空的

 例句 -

Grandma, there is an empty seat.

祖母，這裏有一個空位。

vacant (adj.)

kōng de

空的

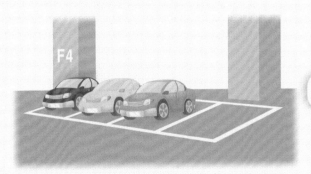

 例句 -

Great! There is still one vacant parking space.

太好了！這裏還有一個空的泊車位。

fast (adj.)

kuài sù de
快速的

 例句 -

High-speed trains are very fast. They can reach more than 300 kilometres per hour.

高速火車的速度很快，時速可超過300公里。

quick (adj.)

kuài sù de
快速的

 例句

Be quick! The green traffic light is flashing.

走快點吧！綠色交通燈正在閃動着。

fly (v.)

fěi xiáng
飛翔

例句 ------------------------------

The plane is flying in the sky.

飛機正在天上飛翔。

glide (v.)

huá xiáng
滑翔

 例句

Gliding through the air is thrilling.

在空中滑翔真是刺激。

forbid (v.)

jìn zhǐ
禁止

182

例句 --------------------------------

Drivers are forbidden from using a hand-held phone while driving.

司機禁止在駕駛時使用手提電話。

prohibit (v.)

jìn zhǐ
禁止

 例句 -

Speeding is strictly prohibited.

嚴禁超速駕駛。

jam (n.)

dǔ sè

堵塞

 例句 -

Dad is stuck in a traffic jam.

爸爸正在塞車。

congestion (n.)

dǔ sè
堵塞

例句

Traffic congestion is very common in most big cities.

交通堵塞在大部分大城市都十分常見。

leave (v.)

lí kāi
離開

 例句 -----------------------------

You are too late. The bus has just left.

你來遲了，巴士剛剛開走了。

bus 的普通話是「公共汽車」。

depart (v.)

lí kāi
離開

 例句

The tourist bus will depart from the hotel at 2 p.m. tomorrow.

旅遊巴將於明天下午兩點離開酒店。

near (prep.)

jiē jìn
接近

 例句 -

He is staying in a hotel near the airport.

他入住的酒店離機場很近。

close (adv.)

kào jìn
靠近

189

 例句 -

Don't get close to the platform gates.

請勿靠近月台幕門。

passenger (n.)

chéng kè
乘客

 例句

The passengers are getting onto the train.
乘客正在登上火車。

traveller (n.)

lǚ kè
旅客

 例句 -

The travellers spent a night at the airport because of the flight delay.

由於航班延誤，旅客在機場留宿了一晚。

reach (v.)

dào dá
到達

192

✦ 例句 -

After a long bus ride, we finally reached the beach.

我們乘坐長途巴士，終於到達了海灘。

 bus 的普通話是「公共汽車」。

arrive (v.)

dào dá

到達

193

 例句 ------------------------

The train will arrive on time.

火車將會準時到達。

rough (adj.)

qí qū de
崎嶇的

194

⟡ 例句 ┈┈┈┈┈┈┈┈┈┈┈┈┈┈┈┈┈┈┈┈┈

It is not possible to ride a bike on this rough road.

在這條崎嶇的路上，並不可能騎單車。

 bike 的普通話是「自行車」。

bumpy (adj.)

diān bǒ de
顛簸的

 例句

The Jeep bounces up and down on the bumpy road.

吉普車在顛簸的路上搖搖晃晃地行駛着。

sidewalk (n.)

xíng rén dào
行人道

196

 例句 -

You may park your bike on the parking rack on the sidewalk.

你可以把單車停放在行人道上的停泊架。

bike 的普通話是「自行車」。

pavement (n.)

xíng rén dào
行人道

 例句 -

You should not ride a scooter on the pavement.

你不應該在行人道上踏滑板車。

stop (n.)

chē zhàn
車站

198

例句

A lot of passengers are waiting for the bus at the bus stop.

很多乘客在巴士站等巴士。

 bus 的普通話是「公共汽車」。

station (n.)

chē zhàn

車站

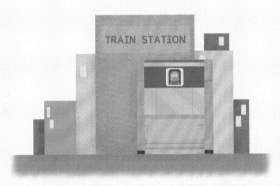

TRAIN STATION

199

 例句 ----------

> station 指較大型的公共交通工具車站,如:火車站、地鐵站。

There is a train station in this district.

這區有一個火車站。

taxi (n.)

<small>dí shì jì chéng chē</small>

的士；計程車

TAXI

200

 例句 -

Taxis are fast and comfortable.

的士又快又舒適。

 taxi 的普通話是「計程車」。

ENG × 粵語　ENG × 普通話

cab (n.)

dí shì　jì chéng chē
的士；計程車

例句

Let's take a cab or we will be late.

坐的士吧，否則我們會遲到。

cab 的普通話是「計程車」。

unsafe (adj.)

bù ān quán de
不安全的

202

例句 --------------------------------

It is unsafe to overload a truck.
貨車超載很不安全。

dangerous (adj.)

wēi xiǎn de
危險的

203

例句

Do not distract the driver. It is dangerous.

不要令司機分心,否則會很危險。

book (v.)

yù dìng
預訂

204

 例句 -

We do not have to line up because I have booked the tickets in advance.

我們不用排隊買門票，因為我提前預訂了。

reserve (v.)

yù liú
預留

The playroom is reserved for the children to have fun.

這間遊戲室是預留給小朋友玩樂的。

boring (adj.)

chén mèn de
沉悶的

206

 例句 -

I kept yawning while watching this boring documentary.

我一邊打呵欠，一邊看這套沉悶的紀錄片。

dull (adj.)

wú qù de
無趣的

207

 例句 ----------------------------

This book is very dull.
這本書很枯燥無趣。

browse (v.)

liú lǎn
瀏覽

208

 例句 -

Let's browse the list of comic books on the site and choose one to read.

我們瀏覽一下網頁上有什麼漫畫，然後選一本來看吧。

休閒

surf (v.)

shàng wǎng

上網

例句

Dad and I surf the Internet to look for some interesting experiments to do.

爸爸和我上網尋找一些有趣的實驗來做。

209

cartoon (n.)

kǎ tōng piàn
卡通片

210

 例句 -

The kids are watching the cartoon attentively.

孩子們全神貫注地觀看卡通片。

animation (n.)

dòng huá
動畫

211

 例句 -------------------------------

He is showing us the animation he made with a computer.

他正在向我們展示他用電腦製作的動畫。

exciting (adj.)

cì jī de
刺激的

 例句 ----------------------------

The kids found this video game very exciting.

孩子們覺得這個電子遊戲很刺激。

thrilling (adj.)

cì jī de jīng xiǎn de
刺激的；驚險的

213

 例句

This roller-coaster is one of the most thrilling rides in the theme park.

這座過山車是主題公園裏其中一個最刺激的機動遊戲。

film (n.)

diàn yǐng
電影

214

✨ 例句 ----------------------------

You should keep quiet when watching a film at the cinema.

在電影院觀看電影時，要保持安靜。

movie (n.)

diàn yǐng
電影

 例句

This adventure movie is family-friendly.

這套冒險電影適合一家大小觀看。

free (adj.)

kōng xián de
空閒的

 例句 -

He goes hiking with friends when he is free.

他空閒時會和朋友去遠足。

spare (adj.)

kōng yú de
空餘的

217

 例句 ------

I do voluntary work in my spare time.

在空餘時間，我會參加義工服務。

funny (adj.)

yǒu qù de
有趣的

218

 例句 -

The clown is so funny.

這個小丑真有趣。

amusing (adj.)

yǒu qù de
有趣的

 例句

We cannot help laughing at his amusing jokes.

他說的笑話很有趣，我們都忍不住哈哈大笑。

game (n.)

bǐ sài
比賽

 例句 - - - - - - - - - -

game 也可指「遊戲」。

The basketball game is on TV now.

電視正在播放籃球比賽。

220

match (n.)

bǐ sài
比賽

 例句 --------------------------------

The boys won the football match.

這羣男孩在足球比賽中勝出了。

hobby (n.)

xìng qù　　shì hào
興趣；嗜好

222

例句

Johnny has many hobbies: playing tennis, cooking, playing the piano, etc.

強尼的興趣很廣泛，包括打網球、烹飪、彈鋼琴……

interest (n.)

xìng qù
興趣

 例句

She has a keen interest in languages. She has learned Putonghua, English, French and Japanese.

她對語言非常感興趣,學習了普通話、英語、法語和日語。

holiday (n.)

jià qī
假期

224

 例句 -

We are enjoying our cruise holiday.

我們正在享受郵輪假期。

vacation (n.)

jià qī
假期

 例句 --------------------------

The beach is packed during summer vacation.

暑假期間，沙灘十分擠迫。

outdoor (adj.)

shì wài de
室外的

 例句 -

At weekends, my parents always do outdoor activities with us.

周末，父母總是會和我們到室外活動。

open-air (adj.)

hù wài de
戶外的

 例句 -

The open-air concert attracted many music lovers.

這個戶外音樂會吸引了很多喜歡音樂的人出席。

photo (n.)

zhào piàn
照片

228

 例句

The tourists are taking photos outside the palace.

遊客正在皇宮外拍照留念。

snapshot (n.)

zhào piàn
照片

229

 例句

Peter is showing us the snapshots he took during his holiday.

彼得正在向我們展示他在假期時拍的照片。

relaxing (adj.)

fàng sòng de
放鬆的

 例句

- -

It is so relaxing to lie on the pool float.

躺在泳池浮牀上，真是讓人放鬆。

chill (adj.)

qīng sòng de
輕鬆的

例句

The chill atmosphere of this coffee shop makes it very popular.

這間咖啡店氣氛輕鬆，大受食客歡迎。

show (n.)

biǎo yǎn
表演

232

 例句 - - - - - - - - - -

show 還有其他意思，
請參看第300頁。

He is rehearsing for his magic show.

他正在排練魔術表演。

performance (n.)

biǎo yǎn
表演

233

 例句

The dance performance is wonderful.

這場舞蹈表演精彩絕倫。

trendy (adj.)

shí máo de
時髦的

 例句

The trendy lady changes her hairstyle frequently.

這位時髦的女士經常轉換髮型。

fashionable (adj.)

shí shàng de
時尚的

 例句 --------------------------------

It is always fashionable to wear jeans.

牛仔褲一向都是時尚之選。

trip (n.)

lǚ chéng
旅程

236

 例句 ----------------------------

We went on a day trip to a local farm last Sunday.

上星期日，我們參加了本地農莊一天遊。

journey (n.)

lǚ chéng
旅程

 例句

The train journey was amazing. We enjoyed the spectacular view very much.

這趟火車旅程十分美妙，我們很享受沿途壯麗的風光。

angry (adj.)

shēng qì de
生氣的

 例句 -

He is very angry because I am late.

他很生氣，因為我遲到了。

furious (adj.)

fèn nù de
憤怒的

 例句 ----------------------------

If mum sees the mess we have made,
she will be furious.

如果媽媽看到我們把東西弄到一團糟，她一定
會很憤怒。

beautiful (adj.)

piào liang de
漂亮的

 例句 -

The princess is beautiful.

這位公主很漂亮。

pretty (adj.)

piào liang de
漂亮的

 例句

I like this pretty dress.
我很喜歡這條漂亮的裙子。

brave (adj.)

yǒng gǎn de
勇敢的

 例句 -

You have to be brave if you want to try bungee jumping.

如果想嘗試高空彈跳，就得勇敢起來。

courageous (adj.)

yǒng gǎn de
勇敢的

243

 例句

The girl is so courageous that she is not afraid of the big dog.

這個小女孩很勇敢，並不害怕大狗。

calm (adj.)

píng jìng de
平靜的

 例句 ----------------------------

The city is very calm late at night.
深夜，這座城市十分平靜。

quiet (adj.)

ān jìng de
安靜的

 例句

We must keep quiet in the library.

我們必須在圖書館保持安靜。

compassionate (adj.)

fù tóng qíng xīn de
富同情心的

  例句

Pansy is compassionate to animals and she has adopted a few stray cats.

潘思對動物富同情心，她收養了幾隻流浪貓。

感覺

 ENG × 粵語　ENG × 普通話

sympathetic (adj.)

fù tóng qíng xīn de
富同情心的

 例句 -

We were sympathetic to our classmate who broke his leg.

同學摔斷了腳，我們都很同情他。

cute (adj.)

kě ài de
可愛的

 例句 -

The newborn kittens are very cute.

剛出生的小貓非常可愛。

lovely (adj.)

kě ài de
可愛的

例句

My little sister looks lovely with her pigtails.

妹妹束着兩條辮子，真是可愛。

eager (adj.)

rè qiè de
熱切的

250

 例句 -

Jenny is eager to receive her friend's letter.

珍妮熱切期待朋友的來信。

enthusiastic (adj.)

rè zhōng de
熱衷的

251

例句

John is enthusiastic about astronomy.
He dreams of being an astronaut.

約翰熱衷於天文學,夢想成為太空人。

happy (adj.)

kuài lè de

快樂的

252

 例句

He feels happy when he plays with his friends.

他和朋友玩樂時,感到很快樂。

cheerful (adj.)

yú kuài de
愉快的

 例句 ----------------------

She always wears a cheerful smile.

她臉上總是掛着愉快的笑容。

hate (v.)

tǎo yàn
討厭

254

 例句

I hate rainy days. I have to stay home all day long.

我討厭下雨天，整天都要留在家。

dislike (v.)

tǎo yàn
討厭

255

 例句 ----------------------------

He dislikes the strong smell of garlic.

他討厭蒜頭濃烈的氣味。

honest (adj.)

chéng shí de
誠實的

256

例句 -

The honest passer-by found a wallet and handed it over to the police.

這位誠實的路人把拾到的錢包交給警察。

frank (adj.)

tǎn chéng de
坦誠的

 例句

To be frank with you, this pair of shoes does not suit you.

坦白說，這雙鞋子並不適合你。

jealous (adj.)

dù jì de

妒忌的

258

 例句

The jealous girl cries when her mum is holding another baby.

當媽媽抱着別人的嬰兒時，這個愛妒忌的小女孩就會大哭起來。

envious (adj.)

xiàn mù de
羨慕的

259

 例句 -----------------------------

The girls are envious of her beautiful new dress.

女生們都很羨慕她身上漂亮的裙子。

kind (adj.)

tǐ tiē de
體貼的

 例句 -

It is very kind of you to offer your seat to the pregnant lady.

你真是體貼，把自己的座位讓給孕婦。

considerate (adj.)

tǐ tiē de
體貼的

261

 例句 - - - - - - - - - -

> considerate 也可指
> 「替人設想的」。

My elder brother is so considerate. He turns off the television while I am studying.

哥哥很體貼，在我溫習的時候，他把電視關掉。

ENG × 粵語

ENG × 普通話

mean (adj.)

kè bó de
刻薄的

262

例句 - - - - - - - - - - - - - - - - - - -

In the story, the stepmother was very mean to Cinderella.

在故事中，後母對灰姑娘很刻薄。

unkind (adj.)

kè bó de   wú qíng de
刻薄的；無情的

 例句 --------------------------------

It is unkind of you to laugh at your friend tripping and falling.

朋友絆倒了，你卻取笑她，你太無情了。

nervous (adj.)

jǐn zhāng de
緊張的

  例句 -----------------------------------

She felt nervous on the first day of school.

上學的第一天，她感到很緊張。

anxious (adj.)

jiāo lǜ de
焦慮的

 例句

The boy gets anxious when he does not see his mum.

當男孩見不到媽媽時，就會感到很焦慮。

sad (adj.)

shāng xīn de
傷心的

所有旅客
All Passengers

 例句

Anna feels sad to say goodbye to her friend.

安娜向朋友道別時，感到很傷心。

unhappy (adj.)

bù kāi xīn de
不開心的

 例句 -

Tim is unhappy because his favourite toy is broken.

小添很不開心，因為他心愛的玩具壞了。

scared (adj.)

hài pà de
害怕的

 例句 ------------------------------

I am scared of bugs.

我很害怕小蟲子。

afraid (adj.)

hài pà de
害怕的

 例句 ----------------------------

The baby is afraid of thunder.

這個嬰兒很害怕雷聲。

感覺

ENG × 粵語　ENG × 普通話

shy (adj.)

hài xiū de
害羞的

270

 例句

The shy boy is not willing to say hello to his new teacher.

這個害羞的男孩不願意向新老師打招呼。

timid (adj.)

xiū qiè de
羞怯的

 例句 - - - - - - - - - - - - - - - - - - -

He wants to ask a question but he is too timid to raise his hand.

他想發問，但是他太羞怯了，不敢舉手。

strange (adj.)

qí guài de
奇怪的

272

 例句 -

Durians smell very strange. I do not like them.

榴槤的氣味十分奇怪，我不喜歡。

weird (adj.)

guài yì de
怪異的

273

 例句 --------------------------

The aye-aye is an animal that looks very weird.

指猴是一種樣子怪異的動物。

工作

ask (v.)

yāo qiú
要求

274

✨ 例句 --------

> ask 也可指「問;請求」。

My supervisor asked me to finish my work by noon.

上司要求我中午前完成工作。

request (v.)

yāo qiú
要求

例句

The customer was not satisfied with the dress so she requested a refund.

顧客不滿意這條裙子，所以要求退款。

boss (n.)

lǎo pǎn
老闆

例句

My boss warned me not to be late anymore.

老闆警告我不要再遲到。

employer (n.)

gù zhǔ
僱主

 例句 -

The employer is interviewing the candidates.

僱主正在對求職者進行面試。

busy (adj.)

máng lù de
忙碌的

 例句 --------------------------

The waiter is busy serving food.

侍應生正在忙於上菜。

hectic (adj.)

fán máng de
繁忙的

 例句 -

The shop assistants have a hectic time during the festive season.

佳節期間，店員都忙個不停。

co-worker (n.)

tóng shì
同事

280

 例句 ------------------

The newcomer is warmly welcomed by his co-workers.

同事熱情地歡迎新入職的同事。

ENG × 粵語 ENG × 普通話

colleague (n.)

tóng shì
同事

281

 例句 -

They threw a party at the office to celebrate their colleague's promotion.

他們在辦公室舉行派對，慶祝同事升遷。

customer (n.)

gù   kè
顧客

 例句 -

The customers are very happy with the food and service of the restaurant.

顧客對餐廳的食物和服務感到很高興。

282

ENG × 粵語

ENG × 普通話

client (n.)

kè hù
客戶

 例句 ------------------------------

She is meeting with her client in the conference room.

她正在會議室會見客戶。

finish (v.)

wán chéng
完成

284

 例句 -

We are having a meeting tomorrow so I have to finish the documents by today.

我們明天要開會,所以我要在今天內完成有關文件。

complete (v.)

wán chéng

完成

 例句

The construction of the footbridge is finally completed.

這座行人天橋的建築工程終於完成了。

found (v.)

chuàng bàn
創 辦

286

 例句 -

The bakery was founded by my late grandmother forty years ago.

這間餅店由我已故的祖母在四十年前創辦。

establish (v.)

chuàng lì
創 立

287

例句

Mr Wong established a design firm after he had graduated from university.

黃先生在大學畢業後，創立了一間設計公司。

💡 工作

hardworking (adj.)

qín fèn de
勤奮的

288

 例句

The hardworking employee always works until late evening.

這位勤奮的僱員經常工作到晚上才下班。

diligent (adj.)

qín fèn de
勤奮的

289

 例句

Mr Chan is a diligent worker who works ten hours a day.

陳先生是一位勤奮的員工，每天工作十小時。

job (n.)

gōng zuò
工作

290

 例句

He loves his job as a bus driver.

他很喜歡巴士司機這份工作。

bus 的普通話是「公共汽車」。

occupation (n.)

zhí yè
職業

例句

Firefighters, doctors and nurses are some of the most respected occupations.

消防員、醫生和護士都是一些最備受尊重的職業。

meeting (n.)

huì yì
會議

292

 例句 -

The secretary was taking notes during the meeting.

秘書在會議上做記錄。

conference (n.)

huì yì
會議

293

 例句 - - - - -

conference 指大型正式會議，通常有一個特定的議題。

The delegates from different countries attended the conference on climate change.

多國代表出席了有關氣候變化的會議。

salary (n.)

xīn jīn
薪金

294

 例句 ---------

salary 多指月薪或年薪。

As a senior manager, he gets a very high salary.

身為高級經理，他的薪金非常豐厚。

wage (n.)

gōng zī
工資

 例句

> wage 多以工時計算。

She earns a decent wage because of her good work attitude.

她工作態度良好，得到可觀的工資。

ENG × 粵語
ENG × 普通話

search (v.)

xún zhǎo
尋找

296

 例句

> search 也可指「搜尋；搜索」。

He is searching the filing cabinet for an important document.

他正在文件櫃尋找一份重要文件。

seek (v.)

xún zhǎo

尋找

 例句 -

If you are seeking jobs, you may go to the job fair.

如果你正在尋找工作，就去一下就業博覽會吧。

send (v.)

fā sòng
發送

例句

My colleague sent me the information by email.

同事用電郵把資料發送給我。

deliver (v.)

dì sòng
遞送

 例句 -

The courier is delivering the parcel.

速遞員正在遞送包裹。

show (v.)

zhǎn shì
展示

300

 例句

show 還有其他意思，
請參看第232頁。

Peter is showing me how to use the
photocopier.

彼得正在向我展示如何使用影印機。

demonstrate (v.)

zhǎn shì
展示

301

 例句 - - - - - - - - - -

> demonstrate 也可指「示範」。

My duty is to demonstrate new products to customers.

我的職責是向顧客展示新產品。

start (v.)

kāi shǐ
開始

302

He will start his new job next Monday.

他下星期一會開始新工作。

begin (v.)

kāi shǐ

開始

303

✦ 例句 ------------------------------

Everyone is here. Let's begin the meeting.

所有人都到了，我們開始會議吧。

stress (n.)

yā lì
壓力

304

 例句 -

He is under a lot of stress because he still has many things to do.

他壓力很大，因為他仍有很多事情要完成。

pressure (n.)

^{yā} ^{lì}
壓力

 例句

The long queue of customers gives the cashier a lot of pressure.

大量顧客正在排隊，收銀員感到很大壓力。

suggest (v.)

jiàn yì

建議

306

 例句

Danny suggested showing the data on a pie chart.

丹尼建議用圓形統計圖來展示數據。

advise (v.)

jiàn yì
建議

 例句 - - - - - - - - -

advise 也可指「勸告」。

I kept sneezing so my supervisor advised me to see the doctor.

我不停打噴嚏，上司建議我去看醫生。

tell (v.)

gào su
告訴

例句 ---------------------------

Can you tell me how to handle this task, please?

請問你可以告訴我這項工作該如何處理嗎？

ENG × 粵語

 ENG × 普通話

inform (v.)

tōng zhī
通知

 例句

This memo is to inform everyone of the fire drill.

這則備忘通知所有人火警演習的安排。

buy (v.)

gòu mǎi
購買

 例句

- -

Mum buys fresh food at the wet market every day.

媽媽每天都去菜市場購買新鮮食品。

purchase (v.)

gòu mǎi
購買

例句

Many household goods can be purchased online nowadays.

很多家庭用品現在都可以網購。

311

ENG × 粵語

ENG × 普通話

cheap (adj.)

pián yi de
便宜的

$90

 例句 -

The watch is only ninety dollars. It is cheap!

這隻手錶只賣九十元，真便宜！

inexpensive (adj.)

jià qián bú guì de
價錢不貴的

$120

 例句 ----------------------------

This vase is inexpensive yet exquisite.

這個花瓶價錢不貴，卻十分精緻。

313

choose (v.)

xuǎn zé
選擇

 例句

We chose this handkerchief for mum.

我們挑選了這條手帕送給媽媽。

ENG × 粵語
ENG × 普通話

select (v.)

tiāo xuǎn
挑選

315

例句 -

The couple is selecting furniture for their new home.

這對夫婦正在為新居挑選家具。

cold (adj.)

hán lěng de
寒冷的

例句

It is too cold to swim in winter.

在冬天游泳實在太冷了。

chilly (adj.)

hán lěng de
寒冷的

317

 例句 ----------------------------

It is chilly. Put on the robe.

天氣很冷，快穿上睡袍。

collect (v.)

shōu jí
收集

318

例句 ----------------------------

I like collecting shells.

我喜歡收集貝殼。

gather (v.)

shōu jí
收集

319

 例句 --------- | gather 也可指「採集」。

The worker is gathering apples from the tree.

工人正在採集樹上的蘋果。

dawn (n.)

<ruby>黎<rt>lí</rt></ruby><ruby>明<rt>míng</rt></ruby>

黎明

 例句 ------------------------

The rooster crows at dawn.

公雞在黎明時分啼叫。

daybreak (n.)

lí míng
黎明

 例句 --------------------------------

If you want to catch the sunrise, you have to wake up before daybreak.

如果想看日出，就要在黎明之前起牀。

disturb (v.)

^{gàn} ^{rǎo}
干擾

 例句 -

Don't disturb me! I am on the phone.

不要打擾我，我正在通電話。

interrupt (v.)

dǎ duàn
打斷

 例句 ----------------------------

It is impolite to interrupt someone when they are talking.

打斷別人說話是很沒禮貌的。

expensive (adj.)

áng guì de
昂貴的

 例句 -

My uncle treated us to an expensive dinner at a fancy restaurant.

叔叔請我們到高級餐廳吃昂貴的晚餐。

pricey (adj.)

áng guì de
昂貴的

$1,000,000

325

 例句

This car is too pricey. Let's go for another one.

這輛車太昂貴了，我們選另一輛吧。

ENG × 粵語 ENG × 普通話

fix (v.)

xiū lǐ
修理

例句 -

Dad is fixing the chair.

爸爸正在修理椅子。

生活

repair (v.)

wéi xiū
維修

327

 例句

The lift is being repaired now. We need to walk up the stairs.

升降機正在維修，我們要走樓梯。

friend (n.)

péng you
朋友

 例句 -

A true friend always listens to you and gives honest opinions.

真正的朋友總是會聆聽你說話,並給予真誠的意見。

pal (n.)

péng you

朋友

329

We have been pals since we were in primary school.

我們從小學開始就已經是朋友了。

get (v.)

shōu dào
收到

330

 例句 -

Dad is glad to get a call from his friend.

爸爸很高興收到朋友的來電。

receive (v.)

shōu dào
收到

 例句 --------------------------------

I received a present from my grandmother.
我收到祖母給我的禮物。

hope (v.)

xī wàng
希望

332

 例句 -

I hope it will be sunny tomorrow.

我希望明天會天色晴朗。

wish (v.)

xī wàng
希望

333

 例句

wish 多用於不可能實現的事。

I wish I could fly in the sky like a bird.
但願我可以像小鳥一樣，在天空中飛翔。

provide (v.)

tí gōng
提供

 例句 -

Drinks and snacks are usually provided on short-haul flights.

短途航班通常都會提供飲品和小吃。

offer (v.)

tí gōng
提供

 例句 ----------------------------

The charity offers clothes and food to people in need.

這個慈善機構為有需要人士提供衣服和食物。

refuse (v.)

jù jué
拒絕

336

 例句 -

He wanted to borrow my bike, but I refused.

他想向我借單車，但是我拒絕了。

bike 的普通話是「自行車」。

reject (v.)

jù jué
拒絕

 例句

Her story was rejected by the publishing house because it was not interesting enough.

她的故事不夠有趣，被出版社拒絕了出版。

rich (adj.)

fù yǒu de
富有的

例句

The rich man donates a lot of money to charity every year.

這位富人每年都向慈善機構捐贈巨款。

wealthy (adj.)

fù yǒu de
富有的

 例句 ---------------------------------

The houses in wealthy neighbourhoods are big and beautiful.

位於富裕社區的屋子又大又漂亮。

talk (v.)

tán huà
談話

✦ 例句 -

They are talking about their favourite activities.

他們正在談論各自最喜歡的活動。

340

speak (v.)

shuō huà
說話

 例句

Hello. Can I speak to Jenny, please?
你好。請問我可以和珍妮談談嗎？

want (v.)

xiǎng yào
想要

 例句 -

Mum, I want this toy car.

媽媽，我想要這輛玩具車。

desire (v.)

kě qiú
渴求

 例句

He is a curious kid who has a strong desire for knowledge.

他是一個好奇心很重的孩子，對知識十分渴求。

wet (adj.)

shī de
濕的

 例句 -

Be careful! The floor is wet and slippery.

小心！地面濕滑。

344

humid (adj.)

cháo shī de
潮濕的

It is humid and warm in spring.

春天的天氣既潮濕又溫暖。

almost (adv.)

jī hū
幾乎

346

例句 -

I am almost done with my homework.

我幾乎完成功課了。

nearly (adv.)

chà bu duō
差不多

 例句 -

The sandcastle is nearly done.

這座沙堡差不多堆砌好了。

big (adj.)

dà de
大的

例句 --------------------------------

Dad caught a big fish.

爸爸釣到一條大魚。

large (adj.)

dà de
大的

 例句

You need a large shopping bag.

你需要一個大購物袋。

ENG × 粵語

ENG × 普通話

each (det.)

měi yí gè
每一個

350

✦ 例句 -

The principal shook hands with each of us.

校長和我們每一個人握手。

every (det.)

měi　yí　gè
每一個

 例句

> every 有「全部；整體」的含義。

Please make sure every window is well closed before leaving.

離開前請確保每扇窗都關妥。

enough (det.)

zú gòu
足夠

 例句 -

Do we have enough chairs for all the children?

我們有足夠的椅子給所有小朋友坐嗎？

sufficient (adj.)

chōng zú de
充足的

 例句

No rush! The class starts at 2 p.m. We have sufficient time.

不用急！課堂下午兩點才開始，我們有充足時間。

formerly (adv.)

yǐ qián
以前

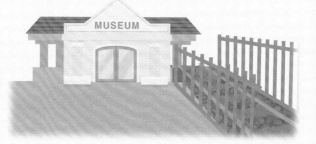

354

 例句 -

This museum was formerly a train station.

這座博物館前身是火車站。

previously (adv.)

zhī qián
之前

 例句 -

Our football coach previously played for the national team.

我們的足球教練之前是國家隊選手。

last (adj.)

zuì hòu de
最後的

 例句 -

Simon was the last pupil to leave the classroom.

西蒙是最後一個離開教室的學生。

final (adj.)

zuì hòu de
最後的

2022 DECEMBER 十二月
31
初九 SATURDAY 星期六

例句

New Year's Eve is the final day of the year.

除夕是一年的最後一天。

many (det.)

hěn duō
很多

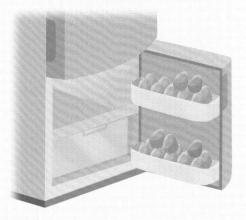

例句 -

There are many eggs in the fridge.

雪櫃有很多雞蛋。

358

✏ fridge 的普通話是「冰箱」。

numerous (adj.)

hěn duō de
很多的

359

 例句

He is a talented actor who has won numerous awards.

他是一位很有才華的演員，贏過很多獎項。

new (adj.)

quán xīn de
全新的

Traditionally, we wear new clothes for Chinese New Year.

按照傳統，我們在農曆新年都會穿上全新的衣服。

unused (adj.)

méi yòng guò de
沒用過的

 例句

If you have any unused stationery, you can donate it to the orphanage.

如果你有沒用過的文具，你可以捐贈給孤兒院。

361

next (adj.)

xià yí gè de
下一個的

362

We need to get off at the next stop.

我們要在下一個站下車。

following (adj.)

xià yí gè de
下一個的

NEXT
3 p.m.

 例句 -

**The following session will start at 3 p.m.
Let's give it a go!**

下一節將於下午3點開始,我們去玩吧!

often (adv.)

shí cháng
時常

 例句

I like reading. I often borrow books from the library.

我很喜歡看書，我時常去圖書館借閱圖書。

regularly (adv.)

jīng cháng

經常

例句 ----------------------------

As a caring owner, he walks his dog regularly.

他是一位很有愛心的主人，經常帶他的狗散步。

reduce (v.)

jiǎn shǎo
減少

366

例句

You should reduce your speed on a wet road.

在濕滑的道路行駛時，應減低速度。

decrease (v.)

jiǎn shǎo
減少

 例句 ----------------------------

Due to the drought, the water level of the reservoir has sharply decreased.

旱情導致水庫的儲水量大幅減少。

same (adj.)

xiāng tóng de
相同的

368

例句 -

We are wearing the same outfits.

我們穿着相同的衣服。

identical (adj.)

yí mú yí yàng de
一模一樣的

 例句

The twins look identical.

這對孿生兒長得一模一樣。

second-hand (adj.)

èr shǒu de
二手的

370

 例句 -

This second-hand table is too old. We cannot give it away.

這張二手桌子太舊了，我們不可以轉贈他人。

pre-owned (adj.)

èr shǒu de
二手的

 例句 ----------------------------

This pre-owned car is very well-maintained.

這輛二手車保養得很好。

seldom (adv.)

hěn shǎo
很少

例句 -

She is very busy so she seldom cooks dinner.

她很忙碌，所以很少下廚煮晚餐。

rarely (adv.)

hěn shǎo
很少

 例句 -

Grandma gets carsick easily. Therefore, she rarely takes a bus.

祖母很容易暈車，所以她很少坐巴士。

bus 的普通話是「公共汽車」。

程度

small (adj.)

xiǎo de
小的

374

 例句 -------------------------------

He was upset that he only got a small slice of cake.

他只得到一小塊蛋糕，感到很不高興。

little (adj.)

xiǎo de
小的

 例句 -

This tank is too little for the fish.

這個魚缸對魚兒來說太小了。

soon (adv.)

jí jiāng
即將

例句 ------------------------------

It looks like it is going to rain very soon.

看來即將就要下雨了。

shortly (adv.)

bù jiǔ
不久

 例句 -

I need to buy some tools. I will come back shortly.

我要去買些工具，很快就回來。

whole (adj.)

zhěng gè de
整個的

378

 例句 ----------------------------

He ate up the whole apple pie.

他吃光整個蘋果派。

entire (adj.)

zhěng gè de
整個的

 例句 -----------------------------

He is cleaning the entire classroom on his own.

他正在獨自打掃整個教室。

wide (adj.)

kuān kuò de
寬闊的

例句 -

The shelf is too wide. It does not fit the room.

書櫃太闊了，房間放不下。

程度

broad (adj.)

kuān kuò de
寬闊的

 例句 ----------------------------

It is enjoyable to drive along the broad country road lined with trees.

在寬闊的鄉間林蔭大道上駕駛，是一件賞心樂事。

新雅兒童英文圖解字典

同義詞

作　　者：Elaine Tin
繪　　圖：歐偉澄
責任編輯：黃稔茵
美術設計：劉麗萍
出　　版：新雅文化事業有限公司
　　　　　香港英皇道499號北角工業大廈18樓
　　　　　電話：（852）2138 7998
　　　　　傳真：（852）2597 4003
　　　　　網址：http://www.sunya.com.hk
　　　　　電郵：marketing@sunya.com.hk
發　　行：香港聯合書刊物流有限公司
　　　　　香港荃灣德士古道220-248號荃灣工業中心16樓
　　　　　電話：（852）2150 2100
　　　　　傳真：（852）2407 3062
　　　　　電郵：info@suplogistics.com.hk
印　　刷：中華商務彩色印刷有限公司
　　　　　香港新界大埔汀麗路36號
版　　次：二〇二三年六月初版

版權所有・不准翻印

ISBN: 978-962-08-8189-3
©2023 Sun Ya Publications (HK) Ltd.
18/F, North Point Industrial Building, 499 King's Road, Hong Kong
Published in Hong Kong SAR, China
Printed in China

作者簡介

Elaine Tin 田依莉

　　持有翻譯及傳譯榮譽文學士學位和語文學碩士學位，曾任兒童圖書翻譯及編輯。熱愛英文教學，喜與兒童互動，故於二零一四年成為英文導師，把知識、經驗和興趣結合起來，讓學生愉快地學習。她認為每個孩子都是獨特的，如能在身旁陪伴和輔助，就能激發他們的興趣和潛質。著有英文學習書《LEARN and USE English in Context 活學活用英文詞彙大圖典》及《中英成語有文化 IDIOMS AND PHRASES》。後者榮獲第三屆香港出版雙年獎「語文學習組別最佳出版獎」。

繪者簡介

Jonas Au 歐偉澄

　　喜歡畫畫、甜品和冷笑話的平凡上班族。

　　目標是可以在發展興趣的同時，能夠應付現在和將來的生活。希望自己的畫作能同時為自己和別人帶來一點快樂和幸福感，透過繪畫留住美好時刻和表達對未來的期盼。

　　目前正在尋找屬於自己的繪畫風格和克服畏高症。